# THE
# Acorn's
# Story

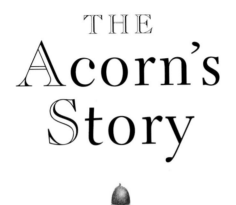

# THE
# Acorn's
# Story

**Valerie Greeley**

MACMILLAN PUBLISHING COMPANY NEW YORK
MAXWELL MACMILLAN INTERNATIONAL
NEW YORK OXFORD SINGAPORE SYDNEY

Who shook me free?
"*I,*" said the breeze,
"*as I rustled the trees.*
*I shook you free.*"

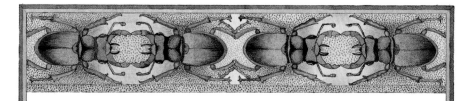

Who tilled the soil?
"*We,*" said the pigs,
"*as we searched under twigs.
We tilled the soil.*"

Who helped me root?
"I," said the rain,
"and it wasn't in vain.
I helped you root."

Who made me green?
"I," said the light,
"when the sun shone bright.
I made you green."

Who watched me grow?
"I," said the mouse,
*"from my cosy house.*
*I watched you grow."*

Who made me strong?
"I," said the earth,
"I broadened your girth.
I made you strong."

W ho made me change?
"We," said the seasons,
"we each had our reasons.
We made you change."

Who broke my bough?
"I," said the lightning,
"my power is frightening.
I broke your bough."

Who heard me cry?
"I," said the owl,
"as I watched the fox prowl.
I heard you cry."

First American edition 1994

Copyright © 1994 by Valerie Greeley

Macmillan Publishing Company is part of the Maxwell Communication Group of Companies.

Macmillan Publishing Company
866 Third Avenue
New York, NY 10022

First published by Blackie Children's Books 1994

Printed in Hong Kong

1 3 5 7 9 10 8 6 4 2

Library of Congress Catalog Card Number: 94-076442

ISBN 0-02-736916-1

Who'll tell my story?
"I," said your seed,
*"for the whole world to read.*
*I'll tell your story."*

First American edition 1994

Copyright © 1994 by Valerie Greeley

Macmillan Publishing Company is part of the Maxwell Communication Group of Companies.

Macmillan Publishing Company
866 Third Avenue
New York, NY 10022

First published by Blackie Children's Books 1994

Printed in Hong Kong

1 3 5 7 9 10 8 6 4 2

Library of Congress Catalog Card Number: 94-076442

ISBN 0-02-736916-1